THE VOYAGE OF
HORACE PIROUELLE

THE VOYAGE OF
HORACE PIROUELLE

PHILIPPE SOUPAULT

INTRODUCTION BY JONATHAN P. EBURNE
TRANSLATED BY JUSTIN VICARI

WAKEFIELD PRESS

CAMBRIDGE, MASSACHUSETTS

This translation © 2023 Wakefield Press

Wakefield Press, P.O. Box 425645, Cambridge, MA 02142

The first three chapters were originally published as *Voyage d'Horace Pirouelle au Groenland* in 1924 in *Les Feuilles libres*, and then all six chapters as *Vie d'Horace Pirouelle* in 1925 by Simon Kra. The final version was published by Lachenal & Ritter in 1983 under the supervision of the author as *Voyage d'Horace Pirouelle* © Editions GALLIMARD, Paris, 1983.

This book was set in Garamond Premier Pro and Helvetica Neue Pro by Wakefield Press. Printed and bound by Sheridan Saline in the United States of America.

ISBN: 978-1-939663-83-2

Available through D.A.P./Distributed Art Publishers
75 Broad Street, Suite 630
New York, New York 10004
Tel: (212) 627-1999
Fax: (212) 627-9484

10   9   8   7   6   5   4   3   2   1

CONTENTS

INTRODUCTION

There is an irresistible fascination about the regions of northern-most Grant Land that is impossible for me to describe. Having no poetry in my soul, and being somewhat hardened by years of experience in that inhospitable country, words proper to give you an idea of its unique beauty do not come to mind. Imagine gorgeous bleakness, beautiful blankness. It never seems broad, bright day, even in the middle of June, and the sky has the different effects of the varying hours of morning and evening twilight from the first to the last peep of day.

—Matthew Henson, *A Negro Explorer at the North Pole* (1912)

L'ACTE GRATUIT

Drafted in 1917 and first published as an excerpt in 1924, Philippe Soupault's *The Voyage of Horace Pirouelle* begins with an exhortation: "A gratuitous act, please." This prompt, or plea, appears as an epigraph to the book's prefatory chapter, under the author's own name.

But it doesn't stop there; each subsequent chapter opens with an increasingly desperate reiteration of that same sentiment, among the novella's many other citational gestures.

A gratuitous act: the term refers to an extreme, even shocking action undertaken without reason, without motive, out of the blue. Even so, the notion of *l'acte gratuit* already bore an imposing literary background by the time Soupault began citing himself in his epigraphs. The term exploded into common usage in the wake of André Gide's 1914 novel *Les Caves du Vatican* (known in English as *Lafcadio's Adventures*), published only months before the outbreak of the First World War. In the novel, Gide's antihero Lafcadio contemplates—and commits—a murder with no rational motive. Having leaped into a burning building to rescue two young children, he later pushes a man out of a train for no reason other than to confirm a kind of radical detachment from moral consideration. For the young French poets of Soupault's generation who began writing in the shadow of the war, Lafcadio's motiveless crime marked a radical breach in European cultural norms that would soon reverberate through the provocations of the Dada movement.

Lafcadio found his complement, moreover, in the *poètes maudits* of the nineteenth century, particularly Arthur Rimbaud, who abruptly abandoned his life as a poet to sell rifles in Ethiopia, and the obscure, Uruguayan-born French writer Isodore Ducasse, the self-proclaimed Comte de Lautréamont, whose *Chants de Maldoror* (1869) featured a criminal antihero who carries out such gratuitous acts on every page. Together with his poet friends, Soupault was among the first moderns to champion the work of these writers as cynosures of poetic experimentation. Soupault's fiction likewise bears the imprint of their imagination. In this regard, the notion of a gratuitous act describes an action that might appear spontaneous but which is in fact self-consciously historical and brimming with significance. The possibility that such acts were not necessarily confined to the imagination, nor safely bound up within the pages of a novel, was likewise of no minor consideration: as the war proved on an almost inconceivable scale, real life could all too easily be ruptured by events that boggled the mind. Some were utterly marvelous; others were unspeakably terrifying. Like Soupault's own experiments in fiction, the gratuitous act was anything but purely random, and far from senseless.

Framed as a Black man's first-person narrative of his travels in the Arctic, *The Voyage of Horace Pirouelle* recounts a series of such gratuitous acts—including the eponymous hero's very decision to set off from Paris to Greenland. Soupault himself had never set foot above the Arctic Circle; Horace Pirouelle's travels are not modeled on the author's own. First conceived and drafted when the author, then an artillery gunner in the French army, was hospitalized for a severe reaction to a typhoid vaccination, *Voyage* is a fantasy of departure. Incidentally, it was during this same period of convalescence that Soupault penned his first published poem, "Départ" (Departure), which appeared in Pierre Albert-Birot's avant-garde magazine *Sic* in 1917. In this light, it's possible to see Horace Pirouelle as both a stand-in for the author's restlessness and as an object of his fascination. Pirouelle is, one might say, an afficionado of the gratuitous act.

A case in point: during the long polar winter, Soupault's titular protagonist whiles away the endless hours of darkness by taking potshots at lights in the dark—which happen to be the oil lanterns of his Inuit neighbors. "In that starless night the lit-up windows of neighboring igloos furnished me with excellent targets." With characteristic sangfroid, Pirouelle narrates the effects of his gunshot fire with neither excitement nor self-judgment, noting simply that the Inuit community attributes the sudden deaths that result from his actions to the demon

Towarsuk. "My neighbors, to explain certain mysterious and sudden deaths accompanied by claps of thunder, agreed that it was a deserved punishment inflicted by Towarsuk, the great devil." This might sound like material drawn from a work of crime fiction, or from the exploits of Lautréamont's Maldoror. Soupault was certainly an avid reader of both.[1] But the source material for the incident is neither a work of fiction nor the murky recesses of the author's imagination; rather, Soupault drew upon Robert Peary's 1910 memoir of his successful North Pole expedition, which was published in French translation in 1912 as *A l'assaut du Pôle Nord* (literally, storming or attacking the North Pole). Here is the corresponding scene from Peary's *North Pole*:

> Any sudden and unexplained barking or howling among the dogs indicates the invisible presence of Tornarsuk [Towarsuk], and the men will run out and crack their whips or fire their rifles to scare away the invader. When, on board the *Roosevelt* in winter quarters, I was suddenly aroused from sleep by the crack of rifles, I did not think there was a mutiny aboard—only that Tornarsuk had ridden by upon the wind.[2]

From Peary's sudden arousal, Soupault has crafted one of Pirouelle's most gratuitous acts. In *The Voyage of Horace Pirouelle* he appropriates Peary's description of how the Inuit community attribute gunfire sounds to the demon Towarsuk—only in the hands of Soupault's protagonist, the shots are fatal.

Many of the episodes in the first chapter of *The Voyage of Horace Pirouelle* are, in fact, drawn from Peary's narrative of his "conquest" of the North Pole; the *Voyage* is pastiche rather than pure invention. Pirouelle's narrative proceeds from the same geographical coordinates as Peary's 1908–1909 expedition to the North Pole, and indeed, the narrative appropriates Inuit terms and names from Peary's snapshots of life among the Inuit communities in Greenland's Smith Sound. The events in chapter 1 shadow the Peary expedition's fall quarters in Etah, West Greenland, whereas the far more fragmentary chapter 2, in the form of journal entries, follows the approximate timeline of the expedition's departure for the pole. The remaining chapters of the novella shift the setting of Pirouelle's exploits from the northwest coast of Greenland to the northeast. Correspondingly, Pirouelle's encounter and subsequent cohabitation with the marooned traveler Henri Simmonet are modeled on Danish explorer Ejnar Mikkelsen's account of the two winters he and his shipmate Iver Iversen spent in a wooden shack above the Artic Circle.[3]

Although *The Voyage of Horace Pirouelle* draws heavily on Peary's *North Pole*, Soupault has made two significant alterations that highlight the core interest, as well as the novelty, of his fictional adaptation. The first is to strike the North Pole entirely from the account. Whereas the attainment of the pole serves as the sole underlying motive for Peary's quest, Pirouelle's journey has neither motive nor telos. In chapter 2, Pirouelle does indeed set out over the ice, with dates that line up with those of Peary's final push across the frozen Arctic Sea; yet in his case there is no attainment of the pole, no "conquest" to which the traveler is inexorably drawn. The chapter ends instead with a final, one-word journal entry: "April 10. Cold." The episode comes to a close, but it does so inconclusively, as if the story itself were suspended in the frozen Artic winter. Echoing Soupault's poem "Départ," *Voyage* is a tale of departure rather than arrival, manifesting a restlessness Soupault elsewhere likened to the spirit of modernity itself.[4]

Second, and even more significantly, Soupault alters the race of his titular explorer: though he borrows from Peary's account, the story shifts its narrative voice from Peary's white, imperial American explorer to the Black law student Horace Pirouelle, born—according to the author's (fictionalized) preface—in Monrovia, the capital of Liberia.

Horace Pirouelle's Blackness is fundamental to Soupault's novella, as central to its approach to storytelling as characteristic of its place in francophone literary and intellectual history. In his "avant-propos" to the narrative, Soupault's authorial or editorial stand-in pontificates at length on his protagonist's Blackness, noting that he was both "the most handsome Negro I have ever met" and also, at times, "a dirty Negro [*un sale nègre*]." Here, Soupault's casual recourse to a racist slur in describing his (alleged) friend is no less alarming than his almost fetishistic attention to Pirouelle's characteristic life-energy, from his "marvelous powers of adaptation" to his "beautiful Negro smile." I will have more to say below about Soupault's treatment of race in the context of Jazz-age Paris; for the moment, suffice to say that it is Pirouelle's Blackness that makes his sudden announcement about traveling to Greenland such a surprise for Soupault's fictionalized white witness. As the latter notes, oscillating between laughter and terror, "an African born below the Equator was touring Greenland! [. . .] This black on that peninsula of ice and snow!" Pirouelle has no reason for going, other than his decision to do so: "Like a lamp," Soupault writes, "[Pirouelle's] heart was empty."

Lest this gesture seem purely gratuitous, however, it's worth noting that neither the sentiment nor the historical precedent of a Black man voyaging above the Arctic Circle is a pure invention, any more than the novella's details about Inuit life.[5] Peary's ultimate attainment of the North Pole in 1909 was achieved by a party of six men: in addition to Peary himself, who could walk only with great difficulty, having lost most of his toes to frostbite in a prior attempt, the group included four Inuit men—Ootah, Egingwah, Seegloo, and Ooqueah—and Peary's longtime assistant, Matthew Alexander Henson

(1866–1955), who was African American. Henson's historic attainment of the pole was, like that of the Inuit members of Peary's party, largely downplayed and all but erased until generations later. Even so, the significance of a Black man braving the fiercest elements of the Arctic winter was lost neither on Peary nor on Henson himself, who published his own memoir, *A Negro Explorer at the North Pole*, in 1912. Unlike Peary's and Mikkelsen's accounts, however, Henson's memoir was never translated into French during either his or Soupault's lifetime, first appearing only in 2021.[6]

Introduced by Peary as "Matthew A. Henson, my negro assistant," Henson is now acknowledged to have been the first of Peary's party to reach the North Pole.[7] In his own account of the 1909 expedition, Henson foregrounds the historical significance of "the fact that Commander Peary's sole companion from the realm of civilization, when he stood at the North Pole, was Matthew A. Henson, a Colored Man."[8] As a citizen of the Jim Crow United States, Henson was well aware that his skill and experience were not only rare—he was one of the few members of Peary's larger expedition outfit who spoke the Inuit language—but also seriously overdetermined in the racialized narratives of imperial power and world-historical precedence that characterized most accounts of Arctic exploration. Peary, in the almost preposterously inflated final lines of his foreword to Henson's memoir, concludes that "it is an interesting fact that in the final conquest of the 'prize of the centuries,' not alone individuals, but *races* were represented. On that bitter brilliant day in April 1909, when the Stars and Stripes floated at the North Pole, Caucasian, Ethiopian, and Mongolian stood side by side at the apex of the earth, in the harmonious companionship resulting from hard work, exposure, danger, and a common object."[9] Henson's own description of reaching the pole is no less world-historical in its claims. As he writes, "Another world's accomplishment was done and finished, and as in the past, from the beginning of history, wherever the world's work was done by a white man, he had been accompanied by a colored man."[10] For Henson, there is nothing gratuitous about his attainment of the pole. It is one of the world's "great works," and its achievement by a man of African descent stood as a testament to racial uplift, as the eminent Black intellectual Booker T. Washington claims in his introduction to Henson's memoirs—if not to racial equity.[11]

For Philippe Soupault as for Henson and Peary, the presence of a Black man in the polar regions was deeply symbolic. Both Henson's and, by extension, Pirouelle's abilities to withstand Arctic conditions provided a counter-discourse to the oft-rehearsed pseudoscientific notion of climatic determinism that proposed that Black people belonged only in the tropical South. In this regard, both the historical person and the fictional character put forward what the scholar Anthony Foy refers to as a "racially synecdochic self": that is, their characters and actions stand not only for the nations they represent as explorers (the United States or, in Pirouelle's case, Liberia), but also for the broader characteristics of an entire race.[12] Henson, a real person, titles his memoir accordingly; Horace Pirouelle, on the other hand, is a fictional character and thus testifies principally to Soupault's own literary and cultural investments.

The Voyage of Horace Pirouelle is *not* a story about Matthew Henson, after all. It would be more accurate to describe it as the story of Soupault's own social fantasies, as well as the author's evolving experiments in writing, amidst the heady atmospheres of the Dada and surrealist movements in Paris in the years after World War I. Even so, *The Voyage of Horace Pirouelle* owes much to Henson's life story, just as Peary's voyage is inconceivable without the labor and experience of his Black and Inuit companions.

*

AUTOMATIC WRITING

> We were … like explorers leaving to discover the world of literature,
> but explorers who were severely appraising the fauna of arts and letters.
> We were prepared to be pitiless.
>
> —Philippe Soupault, *Lost Profiles* (1962)

Philippe Soupault (1897–1990) is perhaps best remembered by literary history as the coauthor, with André Breton, of *Les Champs magnétiques* (*The Magnetic Fields*). Written in 1918 and published the following year, *The Magnetic Fields* is a foundational text for the surrealist movement, which Breton would give formal articulation a few years later in his *Manifesto of Surrealism* (1924). This sequence of prose poems is notable as much for its compositional process as for its startling sequences of images and linguistic combinations. "Prisoners of drops of water," reads the opening line of *Magnetic Fields*, "we are but everlasting animals. We run about the noiseless towns and the enchanted posters no longer touch us."[13] The work was created through the practice known as automatic writing, which would become one of the cornerstones of surrealist poetic activity. Later in his life, Soupault described automatic writing and his collaborations with Breton as an adventure, a kind of exploration made possible by a "pitiless" effort to channel spontaneous thought in written form, free—much like the gratuitous act—from aesthetic or moral preoccupations. As Soupault reminisced in 1963:

> In the course of our research we had noticed, indeed, that, freed
> from all critical pressure and scholarly habit, the mind provided

images and not logical propositions, and that if we were willing to adopt what the psychiatrist Pierre Janet called automatic writing, we would record texts in which we described a "universe" heretofore unexplored. So we decided to give ourselves two weeks to write collaboratively a work in which we prohibited correcting or erasing our "flights of fancy."[14]

For Soupault, this recourse to startling and unorthodox images, as opposed to logical propositions, could open up to a kind of freedom "we had known only in our dreams." At odds with conventional bourgeois reasoning, such freedom did not come easily; it demanded preparation, endurance, and a great deal of literacy. In this regard, it was a bit like polar exploration.

Soupault first met Breton the same year he began writing *The Voyage of Horace Pirouelle*. They were introduced by their mutual mentor and acquaintance Guillaume Apollinaire, from whose play *Les Mamelles de Tiresias* (The breasts of Tiresias)—performed for the first time in 1917—they would later draw the term "surrealism." Together with Breton, the poets Louis Aragon and Paul Eluard, and an expanding group of other young poets and artists, Soupault cofounded the poetry magazine *Littérature* in 1919. This journal formed one of the central points of the Dada movement in Paris, which, over the course of the magazine's four-year lifespan and sparked by collaborations such as *The Magnetic Fields*, would shortly evolve into the surrealist movement.

From the final years of World War I into the mid-1920s, Soupault played a central role in the formation and articulation of surrealism, especially in spurring the group's attention to the "modern spirit" of everyday life in postwar Paris. His early fiction and poetry explore the phenomena of disruption, chance, and mystery at work in modern life, particularly in a rapidly modernizing postwar Paris heady with nightlife, demobilized soldiers, and the explosion of jazz and cinema as popular art forms. At the same time, much of Soupault's writing during this period also abandons Paris in favor of the imagined geography of far-off and explicitly *non*-European places: from travel itself (*La Rose des vents* [Compass Rose], 1920), to Australia (*À la dérive*, 1923), and to the Greenland of *The Voyage of Horace Pirouelle*. This interplay of local and global environments would remain central to Soupault's career as a writer and editor, and, eventually, as a reporter, radio producer, and UNESCO representative—much as it would to surrealism's evolution as an international movement from the 1920s through the present day.

As a text whose initial composition predated *The Magnetic Fields* by nearly a year, *The Voyage of Horace Pirouelle* represents one of Soupault's first forays into automatic writing. Much as Apollinaire's play furnished the surrealist movement's very name, the practice of automatic writing bore an extensive literary genealogy. Certainly, the psychiatric work of Pierre Janet and Sigmund Freud lent it a clinical vocabulary sensitive to the machinations of the human unconscious, even as the practice itself was no less wedded to the mediumistic activities of nineteenth-century mystics and spiritualists—a paradox of which Breton and Soupault were well aware. Yet automatic writing was also powerfully informed by their immersion in the work of writers such as Rimbaud and Lautréamont. For Soupault in particular, this literary genealogy extended to the rapid-fire mash-up of images and ideas characteristic of cheap popular fiction, film serials, and popular music, particularly jazz.

When it appeared in book form in 1925, *The Voyage of Horace Pirouelle* took part in the flurry of publications that accompanied the inauguration of the surrealist movement in Paris, arriving in the months immediately following Breton's *Manifesto of Surrealism* (published in mid-October 1924) and the first issue of the journal *La Révolution Surréaliste* (which appeared in early December 1924). During this same time span, members of the surrealist group published some of their best-known writing: Aragon began serializing the prose reflections that would become *Le Paysan de Paris* (*Paris Peasant*, 1926); Robert Desnos published his own experiments in automatic writing, including the book-length *Deuil pour deuil* (*Mourning for Mourning*, 1924); Paul Eluard published two volumes of poetry, as well as a collection of *152 Proverbs mis au goût du jour* (152 proverbs brought up to date), with Benjamin Péret; another surrealist writer, René Crevel, published two novels (through the publishing house where Soupault worked as editor), *Détours* and *Mon Corps et moi* (Detours and *My Body and I*, both in 1924), and Breton himself published a further work of automatic prose poetry, *Poisson soluble* (*Soluble Fish*, 1924).

The Voyage of Horace Pirouelle was also part of Soupault's own furious burst of literary productivity during this same period. Though he always considered himself a poet first and foremost, Soupault published no fewer than six works of fiction between 1923 and 1925 alone, including the novels *Le Bon apôtre* (The good apostle) and *À la dérive* (Adrift) in 1923, *En joue!* (Take aim!) and *Les Frères Durandeau* (The brothers Durandeau) in 1924, and the shorter fictions *Le Bar de l'amour* and *Voyage* in 1925. Though published as novels or novellas, Soupault referred to these works as "testimonials," on a continuum with his poetry, memoirs, and literary essays.[15] The breakneck pace of his literary activity at this time, which also included work as a magazine editor, book reviewer, and critic, reflected two aspects of Soupault's writing that would lead him further and further away from any direct involvement with surrealism. The first was his approach to automatic writing itself. Though he celebrated the "universe" of imagery it opened up, for Soupault automatic writing had less to do with plumbing the depths of the unconscious than with recombining fragments of popular fiction, newspaper clippings, lines from poetic "prophets" such as Rimbaud and Lautréamont, and personal reminiscences. For instance, in a note published in *La Révolution Surréaliste* in 1925, his final contribution to a surrealist periodical, Soupault invokes Raymond Roussel—the reclusive, oddball author of *Impressions of Africa*—together with Pierre Souvestre and Marcel Allain—the coauthors of the popular *Fantômas* crime serial—as models of automatic writing parallel to those explored in *The Magnetic Fields*. For Soupault, both sets of authors developed startlingly unorthodox writing processes on account of the almost machine-like intensity of their compositional methods. In Roussel's case, this referred to the obsessional formalism of the author's notoriously dense, hermetic abstractions; in the case of the Fantômas authors, it referred to the furious pace of Allain and Souvestre's assembly-line creation of the serial novels, penned during epic writing sessions that lasted up to fourteen hours per day.

The second aspect of Soupault's writing that increasingly pulled him outside the surrealist orbit was his effort to make a living from it. Signing a four-novel contract with the highbrow publisher Bernard Grasset, he continued writing prolifically in order to support himself economically by publishing fiction, as well as poetry and criticism. His 1924 novel *Les Frères Durandeau* was short-listed for the Goncourt Prize, a capitulation to bourgeois taste Soupault found humiliating, later describing his contract for Grasset as "forced labor and lost illusions."[16] The schedule was grueling, no less machine-like than the writing cranked out for the pulps. As Soupault described this work in a later memoir:

I had to write and write … every night until three in the morning. The hard labor of a convict. A life sentence of writing. At this
time I was living a triple life. In waking up in the morning, my
head heavy, I reread what I'd written the night before. I worked
without indulgence but not without reason.[17]

In 1926, Soupault was excluded from the surrealist movement, partly
for his reluctance to join them in reconciling their experimental activities with the revolutionary demands of party communism, but also
for his "triple life"—his increasingly highbrow literary vocation, not to
mention his very busy schedule. He nevertheless continued to write
what he considered to be surrealist works, most notably *Le Nègre*
(The Negro, 1927), *Histoire d'un blanc* (Story of a white man, 1927),
and *Les Dernières nuits de Paris* (1928), translated by William Carlos
Williams in 1929 as *Last Nights of Paris.*

These two aspects of Soupault's approach to automatic writing converge in the final published version of *The Voyage of Horace
Pirouelle*, at once embodied in the restlessness of its eponymous polar
explorer and imprinted stylistically in the terse, even hard-boiled sentences recounting his serial exploits. Compared to Breton's character-
istically long, syntactically complex sentences, Soupault's prose reads
much like a popular crime story.

Between its initial composition in a wartime military hospital in
1917 and its publication by Editions du Sagittaire in 1925, *The Voyage of Horace Pirouelle* bookends the time span of Soupault's direct
involvement in the surrealist movement. Throughout this involvement,
and continuing long after its conclusion, Soupault's string of fictional
works from *Voyage* through *Le Nègre* feature Black heroes or anti-
heroes who embody the author's Rimbauldian "thirst for the infinite."
In place of imperial conquest—the will to domination represented

symbolically by Robert Peary's race to the North Pole and literally by the economic and political engines of colonialism, capitalism, and fascism—Soupault championed the anarchic drive of fugitivity itself. This is the drive articulated by Soupault's literary heroes and embodied, synecdochally, by his Black characters. In addition to Horace Pirouelle, these characters include Albert Martel in the short story "The Death of Nick Carter" (1926), Edgar Manning in *Le Nègre* (1927), and Ralph Putnam in *Le Grand Homme* (The great man, 1929); Soupault also published a book on jazz, *Terpsichore*, in 1928. For this reason, Soupault is often mentioned in accounts of the French *tumulte noir* of the 1920s and early 1930s, in reference to the widespread popularity of all things Black, colonial, and "primitive" among white, European intellectuals and artists during the interwar period. Yet the same period that saw the rise of Josephine Baker and the Revue Nègre in Paris— as well as the nearly endless proliferation of *anthologies nègres* and other European compilations of and commentaries on diasporic Black arts—also witnessed the concentration of Black transnational political and artistic activity in Paris, in dialogue with the Harlem Renaissance and other anticolonial movements. This included, for instance, the *Comité pour la défense de la race nègre*, which began publishing the explicitly revolutionary and anticolonial newspaper *La Race Nègre* in 1927, as well as the influential Black salon organized, together with her sisters, by Paulette Nardal, who would found the *Revue du Monde Noir* in 1930.[18]

This context is important for understanding the politics of race in Soupault's imagination, from Horace Pirouelle onward. On the one hand, Soupault's white narrative witnesses—such as the narrator/editor in the "avant-propos" to *Voyage*—position the author as precisely the kind of French artist fixated on the exoticism or novelty of Black arts and artists. This is an intentional move: Soupault marks his own whiteness explicitly in his early memoir, *Histoire d'un blanc* (1927), published at age thirty in the same year as *Le Nègre*. Soupault considered whiteness, and Europeanness, to be ideologically bankrupt, characterized by an enfeebled will to dominate. Europe, he writes elsewhere, is a "shoddy garden covered with corpses."[19] On the other hand, the Black male protagonists of these works, such as Horace Pirouelle himself, serve as "racial synecdoches" for the kinds of restlessness, antibourgeois imagination, and unrepentant freedom that Soupault sought to channel in his own writing within and beyond surrealism. *Le Nègre*, for instance, celebrates the "absolute liberty" of its titular black antihero, a part-time jazz musician and cocaine dealer, in language reminiscent of the other surrealists' admiration for writers like Lautréamont and Rimbaud—but also with a full-on celebration of the violent gratuitous act. Here is Soupault's narrator, waxing about the proclivities of the Maldoror-like Edgar Manning, in *Le Nègre*:

> I recognize my friend Manning because he is as alive as the color red, and as quick as a catastrophe. He appears and disappears. He moves in a rarified air, in unfathomed waters, in a fire more generous than a lamprey, and he inhabits that noble world punctuated by bursts of laughter and bull's blood.[20]

To define freedom in such a way as to extend to violence and even homicide is a highly vexing proposition. Like Horace Pirouelle, Edgar Manning is an unrepentant killer. What could seem further away from the real political inequalities of race and racism in France—or Liberia, or the United States? In Soupault's imagination, the romanticized characteristics of fictional characters like Pirouelle and Manning become all but indistinguishable from idealized properties of Blackness itself. And although Manning, even more than Pirouelle, is based on a real-life model, such characters are nonetheless *literary* constructions: they testify to the author's predilections and processes—his reading habits, as much as his fantasies of Blackness and his disgust for bourgeois morals and tastes.

Soupault's fictions hardly prescribe homicide as a viable form of liberation or, for that matter, as a racial characteristic. Even so, his work remains provocative—if not easily recuperable—for this very reason. In *The Voyage of Horace Pirouelle*, the homicides Pirouelle carries out among the Inuit community are episodes in the broader journey that serves as his "gratuitous" yet no less powerful driving force. Violence, in this regard, serves as but a medium for the liberatory thirst Soupault's characters relentlessly pursue, rather than the singularly tragic or criminalized outcome of their life stories. To be fearless, pitiless: are these not the real demands of any revolutionary action, such as the anticolonial and antiracist struggles of the twentieth century would demand?

Jonathan P. Eburne

NOTES

1. On Soupault and detective fiction, see Gérard Durozoi, "Philippe Soupault et le roman policier," in *Philippe Soupault: L'ombre frissonante*, ed. Arlette Abert-Birlot, Nathalie Nabert, and Georges Sebbag (Paris: Jean-Michel Place, 2000), 115–122. See also Robin Walz, *Pulp Surrealism: Insolent Popular Culture in Early Twentieth-Century Paris* (Berkeley: University of California Press, 2000), and Jonathan P. Eburne, *Surrealism and the Art of Crime* (Ithaca: Cornell University Press, 2008).

2. Robert Peary, *The North Pole: Its Discovery under the Auspices of the Peary Arctic Club* (Frederick A. Stokes Co., 1910), 64.

3. Mikkelson's memoir, *Lost in the Arctic: Being the Story of the "Alabama" Expedition, 1909–1912*, was published simultaneously in English and French translations in 1913.

4. In a 1927 essay, Soupault writes about Rimbaud in similar terms, explaining that the poet embarked not "on a conquest of the world," but instead "simply pursues his life, and its shadow guides him toward the infinite, the thirst for which is an atrocity, a painful sickness" (Soupault, "A la recherche de Rimbaud," *La Revue nouvelle* [February 1927], in *Littérature et le reste: 1919–1931*, ed. Lydie Lachenal [Paris: Editions Gallimard, 2006], 280.) This "thirst for the infinite" describes Horace Pirouelle's paradoxical motiveless and driving fugitivity, as well as Soupault's ever-present ideas about poetic freedom.

5. Soupault's Inuit terminology—the demon Towarsuk (Tornarsuk), the shamanistic *angakok*, and the temporary madness named as *piblokto*—and most of the Inuit characters named in *Voyage* are drawn from Peary's *North Pole*, which (like Henson's memoir) includes an appendix listing the names of the Inuit inhabitants of Smith Sound, Greenland. In another regard, Soupault's novella intuits—or, perhaps, inventively happens upon—the fact that Henson and Peary both fathered children and cohabited with Inuit women. Though this fact wasn't publicly circulated until the late 1980s, Peary's account elaborates in "ethnographic" fashion on the marriage customs of the local Inuit communities.

6. See Matthew Henson, *Journal d'un explorateur noir au pôle Nord*, trans. Kamel Boukir (Brussels: Zones sensibles, 2021). Boukir's preface addresses the silencing of non-white explorers and researchers in the history of exploration and ethnography alike.

7. Peary, *North Pole*, 20.

8. Matthew Alexander Henson, *A Negro Explorer at the North Pole* (Frederick A. Stokes Company, 1912), 2.

9. Peary, "Foreword," in Henson, *A Negro Explorer at the North Pole*, viii.

10. Henson, *A Negro Explorer at the North Pole*, 136.

11. Booker T. Washington, "Introduction," in Henson, *A Negro Explorer at the North Pole*, xv–xx.

12. Anthony S. Foy, "Matthew Henson and The Antinomies of Racial Uplift," *Auto/Biography Studies* 27, no. 1 (2012): 19–44; 22–23.

13. André Breton and Philippe Soupault, *The Magnetic Fields*, trans. David Gascoyne (London: Atlas Press, 1985), 25.

14. Philippe Soupault, *Lost Profiles: Memoirs of Cubism, Dada, and Surrealism*, trans. Alan Bernheimer (San Francisco: City Lights, 2016), 17.

15. Philppe Soupault, V*ingt mille et un jours: entretiens avec Serge Fauchereau* (Paris: Belfond, 1980), 21.

16. Soupault, *Vingt mille et un jours*, 21.

17. Philippe Soupault, *Mémoires de l'oubli 1923–1926* (Paris: Lachenal & Ritter, 1986), 133.

18. On translational Black intellectual life in Paris between the wars, see, for instance, Brent Hayes Edwards, *The Practice of Diaspora: Literature, Translation, and the Rise of Black Internationalism* (Cambridge, MA: Harvard University Press, 2003); T. Denean Sharpley-Whiting, *Negritude Women* (Minneapolis: University of Minnesota Press, 2002); Gary Wilder, *The French Imperial Nation-State: Negritude and Colonial Humanism between the Two World Wars* (Chicago: University of Chicago Press, 2005); Phyllis Taoua, *Forms of Protest: Anti-Colonialism and Avant-Gardes in Africa, the Caribbean, and France* (London: Heinemann, 2002). On the French reception of Black art and artists, see, for instance, Petrine Archer-Straw, *Negrophilia: Avant-Garde Paris and Black Culture in the 1920s* (London:

Thames and Hudson, 2000); and Tricia Danielle Keaton, T. Denean Sharpley-Whiting, and Tyler Stovall, eds., *Black France/France Noire: The History and Politics of Blackness* (Durham: Duke University Press, 2012).

19. Philippe Soupault, "Vanité de l'Europe," *Les Cahiers du mois* 9–10 (February–March 1935): 64–68; 67.

20. Soupault, *Le Nègre*, unpublished translation by Randall Cherry, 30.

FURTHER READING

Books by Philippe Soupault in English

Age of Assassins: The Story of Prisoner No. 1234. Trans. Hannah Josephson. New York: Knopf, 1946.

The American Influence in France. Trans. Babette and Glenn Hughes. Seattle: University of Washington Bookstore, 1930.

I'm Lying: Selected Translations of Philippe Soupault. Trans. Paulette Schmidt. Providence, RI: Lost Roads, 1985.

Last Nights of Paris (1928). Trans. William Carlos Williams. Cambridge, MA: Exact Change, 1992.

Lost Profiles: Memoirs of Cubism, Dada, and Surrealism. Trans. Alan Bernheimer (City Lights Publishers), 2016.

The Magnetic Fields. (With André Breton.) Trans. David Gascoyne. London: Atlas Press, 1985.

The Magnetic Fields. (With André Breton.) Trans. Charlotte Mandell. New York: NYRB, 2020.

Ode to Bombed London. Trans. Norman Cameron. Algiers: Charlot, 1944.

William Blake. Trans. J. Lewis Blake. New York: Dodd, Mead, 1928.

On Matthew Henson and Polar Blackness

Blum, Hester. *News from the Ends of the Earth: The Print Culture of Polar Exploration*. Durham, NC: Duke University Press, 2019.

Counter, S. Allen. *North Pole Legacy: The Search for the Arctic Offspring of Robert Peary and Matthew Henson*. New York: Skyhorse Publishing, 2018.

Henson, Matthew. *A Negro Explorer at the North Pole*. New York: Frederick A. Stokes Company, 1912. (French translation: *Journal d'un explorateur noir au pôle Nord*. Trans. Kamel Boukir. Brussels: Zones sensibles, 2021.)

Johnson, Mat. *Pym*. New York: Spiegel & Grau, 2011.

Kpomassie, Tété Michel. *An African in Greenland* [1981]. Trans. James Kirkup. New York: NYRB, 2001.

A gratuitous act, please.

PHILIPPE SOUPAULT

Another mark of servitude is the attitude of modern thought in regard to facts. In some respects, it becomes the slave of hard facts, in the sense that scholars and historians tend to transform it into a kind of recording cylinder on which all facts great and small are registered. Apart from material fact, no truth. Intelligence succumbs to erudition, and to a quantity of knowledge it becomes incapable of discerning and judging.

JACQUES MARITAIN

THE LIFE OF HORACE PIROUELLE

I knew Horace Pirouelle about ten years ago. I don't believe I'm wrong in declaring that he is the most handsome Negro I have ever met. He was taking courses in Roman law and civil law at the Faculté de Paris.

We would frequent the same café.

The waiter, if I remember right, was named Albert. Albert had a little mustache that looked like letters of the alphabet. He was nonchalant: his drooping eyelids invited customers to sleep, to dreams and drunkenness. Albert would say: "I knew a little lady (he'd click his tongue), I knew a little blonde lady." Then he'd tell a naïve story. The little blonde, after loving him for two or three days, cheated on him.

Horace Pirouelle would light an English cigarette, drink his café crème, and smile with all his white Negro teeth. My friend Horace was in fact born in Monrovia, the capital of the Republic of Liberia.

Ah the ironies of life! It would rain, my friend Horace would be happy, and when by chance snow fell my friend Horace would smile, smile, and smile.

His smile was not cynical, nor sarcastic, nor wicked, nor deceptive, nor conventional, nor ironic, nor stupid, nor professional. It was the beautiful Negro smile of one happy to be alive and to get drunk, not on words but on liquor. When the Earth seemed to turn too quickly to his liking, he would then look for motives, desires, and grow immoderately sad. Heaven was evil and Horace renounced the faith of his fathers.* The pitcher will go to the well once too often . . .

How astonished others seem to be by such a straightforward way of living! Life is life, I will admit—but I don't want to discuss here the unique meaning of life, the train of thought, or the content of dreams—I am, today, the biographer of Horace Pirouelle who was my friend, my classmate, and a diligent student as well as a devoted and charming friend of whom I have retained the fondest memories.

Oh memory, oh recollection!

The light slowly fades. In the distance a very heavy murmur can be heard scraping the earth, scorching in its passage the illusions of animals without sorrow. Nearer by, sky touches earth: a spark bursts forth and it is the

---

* Pirouelle was at that time a Protestant.

sun, beautiful as the gaze of God. I can make out before me the shadow of a man who yanks despairingly at the levers of a machine. A small bird perches on his fingers. He awaits a phenomenon, a catastrophe, a miracle. Only the vast murmur responds, and I hear it, this great noise I shall soon probably see, for it seems to burst my ears, to beat at my temples. No, perhaps I need to close my eyes so as not to go pale, so as not to marvel at my own existence of which this murmur, which I believe to be immense, is but an echo. I also wait, like the sturdy little bird, like the shadow, my own shadow, I lie in wait for my mystery, the forward march of a man who is myself, neither poor nor rich but uncomplicated, me.

Memory serves me well and dictates these images to me. I can't get carried away as I remember Horace Pirouelle. At times he was a dirty Negro. Human relationships are full of conflict.

I find it quite difficult to characterize this young man.*

After receiving his primary education in Monrovia from Protestant missionaries, the young Horace

---

* Horace Pirouelle was energetic, tenacious, educated, intelligent, profoundly honest, scrupulously so, and above all lacking any vanity and selfishness. The humble earned all his care and good wishes: Pirouelle was harsh only toward those who do not benefit the world with the treasures invested in them by their genes, their luck, and their skills.

Pirouelle was sent to lycée Condorcet to continue his studies, then to law school in Paris. He then went to work for one of his uncles, a fat grocer, and soon became an associate. He was twenty-five years old. He saved up money.*

He was never homesick. He had purchased a little two-seater car and, in the evening when the store closed, he would leap behind the wheel and go to dine at Saint Germain, at Versailles, at Rambouillet, at Sceaux, or at Mantes. He would drive fast, and when he cleared the gates of Paris, he would floor the accelerator.

One evening, I ran into him in Place de la Concorde. At his side was a blonde, a little blonde who smiled from ear to ear. There was nothing tragic about this adventure. It didn't end in marriage, suicide, or crime. After the little blonde called Thérèse came a little brunette they called Lili. Every evening, Horace and Lili would dine in the neighborhoods of Paris, in Saint Germain, in Versailles ... Horace was happy.

I was astonished. By the light of a lamp, I dreamed of that simple happiness, that quotidian joy, winged, of genuine worth. The fire, a rooster, died in the hearth, and I no longer knew what to say, what to do. The shadow of

---

* A significant amount of money. The food industry is a fruitful one. It is, said an economist in our circle of friends, proof of the decadence of the European industrial mind.

happiness stretched across the ceiling. I didn't dare look at myself in a mirror. A simple look at the man who lets his soul wither without screaming out. All the violins of heaven and the songs of the angels could not console someone who waits by a deathbed or by a fireplace. Acknowledgments, monologues, discourses, laments, nothing is worth as much as a dignified and profound silence.

Horace was happy . . . I could only note his marvelous powers of adaptation. Life is a woman you must love. Let others than me jeer. Horace was profoundly happy. In the evening, after the store closed . . .

It was on one of those evenings (I was writing my first novel, *The Good Apostle*) that Horace Pirouelle phoned me. He stopped by. I read a decision in his eyes. He was still smiling, but in this smile were pride, courage, disdain, noblesse. "My dear friend," he said to me after taking off his gloves, "my dear friend, I have some big news . . ." During the silence that ensued I made a supposition: "He's getting married," I thought. "Bravo!" Mistakes always leap to hand, like penholders. I lack imagination, that's a fact. There is no way to combat this flaw. And then romanticism . . .

"My dear friend, I have some big news . . ." He fell silent and I smiled: I thought I had guessed it. I took my hand out of my pocket to shake his. He went on: "I'm going to Greenland!" Surprise! I burst out laughing. That, as they say, was too much: Horace Pirouelle, citizen of the Republic of Liberia, Negro, grocer, motorist, lover, and paralegal was becoming an explorer! That at least is what I imagined, and I was not at all wrong. He told me more about his plans without sparing me any details. Though I had laughed, I was now terrified. An African born below the Equator was touring Greenland! Horace was joking!—and to convince myself of it, I burst out laughing again. That Black man on that peninsula of ice and snow!* One never laughs without a reason. I recognized this today.

Horace was not leaving because of a disappointment in love, a gambling debt, or disillusionment. For hours he explained to me all the reasons he could not put forward. I understood that he was going simply to go. A true voyager, as Baudelaire once said. Like a lamp his heart was empty. He had no reason to remain in Paris and no motive for departing. His decision was made. His character obliged him to leave and not stay. If one truly wished to, one could divide human beings into two categories: those who, having no reason to stay or to go, leave, and those who, also totally bereft, remain at a standstill.

Horace was not curious. He was going to Greenland the way someone prefers a symphony to a quartet. Names and numbers hold a mysterious power. The word

---

* This is an error. I learned this since. Greenland is not covered in ice and snow as I had thought.

"Greenland" signified mystery. Horace was still too young to disregard that call. Mystery and vertigo.

Horace was not romantic. Neither the *supreme adieu of handkerchiefs*, nor the bleating of ships, nor the land one leaves behind ... He preferred to say: "I'm leaving." One should never be surprised by such a decision. When I think about it, it seems natural to me. How many of us live in cities, unastonished, as tranquil as can be? How many of us could never stand such a life? Far be it for me to justify my friend's departure, farther still to explain it. Justifications and explanations are like scratching.

So Horace Pirouelle went, proud and content. He sold his little car and made some preparations. That, at least, was necessary. A few sweaters, precise information, and maps.

One evening around 7:17 I shook hands with him on Platform 19 of the Gare du Nord. Lili was at my side.

Leaving the station, the weather was beautiful, I went to sit on the terrace of a café.* I was truly alone, nearly disoriented.

They brought me a cognac with water and, by mistake, the train schedule. I watched, as an herbivore must, the tramways and buses. The taxis stood in queue. My hands were empty. The weather was beautiful, really very beautiful, and I was truly very much alone. My glass was

---

* The Terminus Denain, dear to my dear Paul Éluard.

full of a blond alcohol and I distractedly lit one of my cigarettes.* Numbers galloped beneath my skull. I needed consoling. I felt dense, so dense, as they say, you could cut it with a knife. My usual courage, which I always recognized by a pressure in my hands, had deserted me.

If I talk a lot and offhandedly about the evening of that day, it is because it seems to me that the life of Horace Pirouelle would be incomplete if I did not speak of his absence.

I had no courage; I wasn't hungry or thirsty. Just the desire for a show, any sort of show. I wasn't thinking of Horace Pirouelle—nor the voyage, or the Voyage; no, I was really thinking only of myself all alone, seated on a rattan chair, before a table made of iron and marble, before a glass of liquor into which I was about to pour some water. I poured the water and drank. And the streetlights were lit, and the flame was motionless and the street, like a river, trundled necessarily anonymous faces. All at once one of those faces dictated a name to me: "Julien . . ." But that's another story, another beautiful story, another very beautiful story.

Philippe Soupault, 1925

---

* I enjoy smoking "Pirate" cigarettes.

THE VOYAGE OF HORACE PIROUELLE

Just one gratuitous act, please.

PHILIPPE SOUPAULT

I have a simple beauty and that's lucky
I glide along the roof of winds
I glide along the roof of seas
I've grown sentimental
I no longer know the conductor
I no longer move silk on ice floes
I'm sick flowers and pebbles
I love the most Chinese of nudes
I love the most nude of bird swoops
I'm an old woman but here I am beautiful
And the shadow that descends from deep windows
Spares each evening the black heart of my eyes

PAUL ÉLUARD

I

———

On 18 November, I turned twenty-five, I left for Greenland. At the station a few friends came to shake my hand and wave theirs the moment the train started up. A good crossing. Two months later I arrived at Etah, a small port bathed by Baffin Bay. I stayed only three days in that village where four or five Danes sold alcohol, corned beef, and blue sunglasses. I liked walking along the avenues bordered with miniature stunted trees. Then I went deeper into Greenland.

It was summer. Every evening I used hand gestures to politely ask some Eskimo to take me in for the night; in the morning I continued my way accompanied by several dogs who abandoned me one by one. Around noon one day I spotted a mountain which I named Mont Pirouelle at the foot of which sat a sizable encampment of tents. Some men approached me and asked me very cordially to come inside their dwelling which was covered with seal and walrus skins. They kept calling this dwelling a tupik. They offered me dried fish and showed me a place to sleep. The next day and every day after that, I went out hunting with them.

In the evening we gathered under a big tent, and I listened to my friends talk as they polished their weapons of ivory and bone and fashioned arrows. They introduced me to their wives, who wore the same clothing as they did: they dress in tunics and pants of bearskin or dogskin. At the beginning of my stay, it was difficult for me to stay in their home which was dominated by a powerful stench. Every night, in tall vases of schist, they burn baleen whale oil, which spreads an odor very disagreeable to those not used to it and who likewise don't care for the aromas emanating from the dried fish, the hunks of meat, and the turds that the men, women, and dogs leave about.

A few weeks went by, and I began to express myself rather elegantly in their dialect. One morning I went

PHILIPPE SOUPAULT

by mistake into a tent that was not mine. A woman was washing up. She leaned over a big tub filled with urine which she splashed upon her face and her breasts. She did not let out a cry but looked at me. I stood there in front of her, saying nothing, only admiring her clear yellow skin, her thick hair straight and black, her wide face with her protruding cheekbones, her slanted and barely open eyes, her elongated and exceedingly high skull. In short, she looked good to me. I lived with Tookoomah after that.

In mid-August we hiked to a prairie around the foothills of Mont Pirouelle. Some caribous were passing in the very tall grass and only raised their heads to watch us pass, opening their big eyes. Tookoomah gathered dandelions and saxifrages which she brought to her nostrils and then gave to me. Flies and bumblebees murmured around my companion. We didn't wait for the sunset since it wouldn't take place for another seventeen days. We went back to our dwelling and on the way there I admired those charming flowers that have no scent.

A guy named Ootah showed up one day at the door of our tupik. He came, he said, to get Tookoomah back under the insulting pretext that she didn't suit me. I had gotten accustomed to this woman's caresses and wasn't interested in changing anything. We went looking for Tookoomah's father.

While the old man calculated and his daughter smiled, Ootah tried to prove his might by seizing me in his arms, lifting me over his head and holding me in that pleasant position for as long as he could. When he'd had enough, he set me back on the ground and I had to follow his example. I was declared the winner, and the father told me to go and sleep with his daughter since I was the worthiest of her embraces and her sighs.

Winter approached, and every day Tookoomah would speak to me about the move near at hand, the igloo we would live in, her bearskin pants, and especially her dog-skin tunic. At the end of September, snow began to fall; we left our tent and chose an igloo with a solid roof. Our winter abode was built of stone covered with snow and sealskin. One entered it through a tunnel three or four meters long and the only daylight was through a small window covered with the intestinal membranes of seals. I carried over some furniture as well as my clothing and my weapons.

From time to time during the vigil, which lasted for about a hundred days, my friends would come over. An old man would rise and declaim a poem, each verse of which was repeated by all those present. I have unfortunately retained only the one they recited most often and which they entitled: *Snow*.

> Time
> Wind
> Mountain
> Igloo
> Flame
> Eye
> Flame
> Igloo
> Mountain
> Wind
> Time

My neighbor Ikwah seemed to like me a lot. Nearly every day he would bring me little presents: caribou feet, locks of his father's hair, seals' eyes. He would pull on my hair which had gotten very long, assuring me of his friendship. He also liked to pinch me. We would spend long hours together.

Tookoomah's sister, Elatoo, often came to see us, bringing her very young son. She would take off her clothes and start talking. But her child would bother her and she would entrust him to me. Then she would start talking again, explaining with numerous details and long-winded comments the fights between her husband and her father, enumerating blows given and received. Sometimes she burst out laughing when describing the recent bump adorning her father's forehead. Throughout her accounts the child would suddenly scream.

During that long night of around two hundred and forty hours I slept a lot. Still, this activity could hardly fill the night. I sharpened my weapons and polished my revolver. From time to time I tore through the window and practiced my shooting. In that starless night the lit windows of neighboring igloos provided excellent targets. I got quite good. My neighbors, to explain certain mysterious and sudden deaths accompanied by claps of thunder, agreed that it was a deserved punishment inflicted by Towarsuk, the great devil.

I displayed light skepticism regarding the tribe's beliefs; I could not take seriously the wrath of the great devil Towarsuk who so frightened my kinsfolk and friends. My attitude outraged someone named Kyoahpaldho. This man performed the duties of shaman or more precisely angakok. These duties consisted of contorting himself while screaming and relentlessly pounding on a walrus's bronchial membrane stretched over an arc-shaped bone. He claimed to cure any illness by this method.

Smiling, he came to get me so that I could hear the great devil cry out. I dressed in a hurry and crawled out of the igloo. He groped for my hand as the wind blew snow and spurred us on. We walked into the night. Ten minutes after our departure, snow began to fall, and I felt flakes land on my face. I followed him without making any fuss. Suddenly I heard a dog howling in the distance. We continued to walk without speaking or seeing each other. From time to time we stopped to shake off the snow that covered us. And again, a dog howled, but I could not make out where it was in relation to us. My companion didn't stop and maybe even started walking faster. It must have been an hour since we had set out. He stopped me when I heard the dog howl for the third time, but closer.

Kyoahpaldho continued on and I had to quicken my pace to keep up with him. At that moment we were struggling against the wind and the snow squalls.

I was startled by a long whistle, to which my companion whistled back. A few minutes later I felt a dog around my legs and heard his rapid panting. I asked Kyoahpaldho what he thought about the arrival of the dog, but I got no reply.

I was knocked over and fell on my back. A man grabbed my legs and held them down as Kyoahpaldho strangled me, screaming: "Towarsuk, Towarsuk!" I dug in my pocket and grabbed my revolver.

To get back home I followed the dog.

A few days later they came to ask me where the shaman was. I replied: "Lost ..."

Despite how cold it was at that time, I was rarely sick. All at once I contracted a violent flu after a curious atmospheric phenomenon. A fierce south wind blew for several hours, whirling monstrous snowflakes about as the temperature climbed from –25 degrees (Fahrenheit) to +43 degrees. Naturally, my companion ran to get help. A few of the shamans were courageous enough to care for me. They set up their little drums around my bed and for over fifteen minutes screamed and drummed as they gesticulated. I'd seen this remedy applied frequently and with success. But my fever did not break. I did recover though, and the observations I made about that storm prompted me to write up a few meteorological, oceanographic, and astronomical findings.

I observed first that the phases of the moon were regular and that only the trajectory it followed in the sky was abnormal; I established that it shone on us roughly ten days out of thirty. This lunar light allowed us to go out and hunt caribou, bear, or musk ox. It gave to the group a semblance of activity. The wives exchanged skins and their husbands weapons; sometimes a blasé husband exchanged a stupid wife for a cantankerous one. Her delighted parents nodded to show encouragement and assent.

*

One night I was awakened by piercing cries. I saw my companion Tookoomah screaming and tearing at her clothes in the middle of the igloo. She spun in a circle then began to pace back and forth while crying hot tears. One by one her clothes came off. When she was completely naked, she jumped, gesticulated, then suddenly ran outside. I followed her, a bit surprised, and in the lunar brightness I saw her roll on the ground, run about, tear at her hair, and emphasize her howling with obscene gestures without even caring about the temperature which was at that time around −40 degrees (Fahrenheit). She was agitated for twenty minutes, began to cry and, calmer, returned to her dwelling. Her eyes were bloodshot and her body was shaking with chills. Out of curiosity I took her pulse and noted that it was very elevated.

A few days later I told her that one of her friends had been strangely ill and I gave her all the details. She smiled without seeming surprised and replied that it was "piblokto."

*

Near the end of January, the 28th, I believe, around noon, I noticed a faint red glow in the southern sky. Winter was over. Immediately I went to work, for I wished to put certain plans into motion as quickly as possible. With the help of several neighbors, I built two sleds and fashioned dog harnesses from sealskin. When I finished all these preparations, I loaded hunks of meat and dried fish onto the sleds. My friend Ikwah wanted to accompany me and took up the second sled. On 14 February everything was ready.

We left as soon as the sun rose above the horizon. I wanted to explore the northern shore of Greenland. I soon saw that it would be impossible for me to carry out this expedition due to the enormous quantity of fjords that border Washington Land and Hall Land. So I decided to cross Greenland from west to east at the latitude 80 degrees north. My companion, who seemed determined to follow me to the very end, was a skilled hunter and an excellent hiker.

Just one little gratuitous act, please.

PHILIPPE SOUPAULT

Now let's set out for the house of seaweed
where we shall see elements covered by their shadow
to creep up like criminals
to destroy tomorrow's passenger
oh my friend my dear fear

BENJAMIN PÉRET

II

———

On 14 February, we leave the outskirts of Mont Pirouelle.

The flat and even ground soon grows rugged. Chains of hillocks.

To cross these bulges, we have to carry the sleds for a fairly long distance.

This stage is seven kilometers.

Our little tent is barely big enough to shelter the two of us.

We advance rapidly over the great level plains. At the end of the day, heaps of snow make for a slow and painful porterage of the sleds. Nine kilometers covered. In the following days, the ground is dead level and we often cover more than fifteen kilometers.

20 February

Sunshine. Superb weather but intensely cold, especially at night.

21 February

At nine o'clock this morning, very low temperature.

22 February

From eleven-thirty in the morning until eight in the evening we traveled over twenty-one kilometers.

26 February

The ground grows very rugged. At every step there are chains of hillocks over which we have to carry our sleds. We kill a sick dog who could no longer keep up and toss the cadaver to its comrades.

2 March

More chains of hillocks.

3 March

Very slow progress.

8 March

A lot of time lost crossing heaps of ice.

Yesterday after a rest the northeast wind picked up and the sky got overcast.

14 March

Under the influence of a southern wind the temperature climbs rapidly.

PHILIPPE SOUPAULT

21 March

A storm from the south. The terrain gets worse and worse.

26 March

Another dog is sacrificed.

31 March

Snow.

4 April

Cold.

10 April

Cold.

I'm asking for just one little gratuitous act, please.

PHILIPPE SOUPAULT

The name of Casimir Bullet belonged to him only because he had taken it, and it was to his liking because after having considered it for a long time he found it ridiculous.

COMTE DE GOBINEAU

III

———

It had been about two months since we set out when one evening at sunset Ikwah spotted an igloo and let out a cry. He shared this discovery with me, and I was rather surprised to see how completely isolated this dwelling was. As much as I tried, I could not make out any other abodes. We got the dogs moving and ten minutes later I arrived at the entrance to this igloo. We unharnessed the dogs who sat near the sleds.

We looked through the little window into the igloo and saw an old man with a big beard and long hair. I did not know what language to use to ask him for hospitality and was about to address him in English when just like that he said to me: "Bonjour." He shook Ikwah's hand and asked us to come into his dwelling. I was very surprised to see that in that warm season he still lived in an igloo and not a tent as Eskimo custom dictates.

✴

He had us stretch out and open a can of peas, which we ate hungrily. He put on his eyeglasses to examine us close up and in detail, but without saying a word. When we had emptied the can of peas he got a glass, which he filled with whisky and held out to me. He offered it to my companion who was more suspicious and refused it. The old man didn't insist and set the bottle down by the bed I was in. After looking at his watch, he stretched out a bearskin on the ground and went to sleep without wishing us goodnight. He didn't even put out the candle.

✴

The following morning when I woke, I saw our host getting dressed. He slowly combed his long white beard while staring at the small translucent window. He did not seem to hear Ikwah snoring or take any note of my movements. From time to time his comb fell to the ground and, without taking his eyes off the little window, he groped around and picked it up again.

He took up a walking stick and went out. I could, at my ease and half asleep, examine the interior of that igloo. It was a relatively spacious room, lit by the single

PHILIPPE SOUPAULT

small window. Rows of tin cans in all shapes and sizes were stacked on top of each other, forming a multicolored tapestry against the walls from which a few gold medallions glittered. Two or three empty bottles, bearskins, a watch made up all the furnishings. I saw no maps, no books, no photographs. I gathered up some crumpled sheets of paper and unfolded them. He had drawn uppercase letters and geometric figures all over them.

✳

After two hours the old man returned, rubbed his hands together, and sat down. I asked him where we were, and he told me: "At latitude 81 degrees north in Mylius Erichsen Land between Independence Fjord and Danmark Fjord." I opened my map of Greenland and he pointed to the precise spot with his very long fingernail. I thanked him and told him that I had come from the vicinity of Humboldt Glacier at latitude 79 degrees north. He didn't reply and I decided to stop talking. Ikwah was clearly exhausted and continued to snore loudly.

✳

I went out in turn without waking my companion. I rummaged in the sleds for meat to feed to the dogs. I sliced off several bits which I planned to eat myself. Having finished I looked around. The dwelling stood in the middle of a plain and I couldn't figure out why anyone would have chosen that locale. Absolute indifference would seem to have guided such a choice. When I went back into the igloo I saw Ikwah eating tinned lobster with evident pleasure while the resigned old man chewed slowly and mechanically.

We remained silent that whole first day. Only Ikwah spoke a little, asking our host for his name, if he had killed many bears, and where his wife was. The old man almost never replied and often seemed not to listen. He lay stretched out, his eyes shut. A nervous twitch subtly deformed his face. Sometimes he got up and in one gulp emptied a glass of liquor with eyes half closed.

My companion gave him a despairing look.

The next morning when he reached for his walking stick, I was already dressed and left at the same time he did. I followed him without him noticing, or at least without seeming to be aware of my presence. After we had walked for ten minutes, I decided to speak to him: "Bonjour," I said. He didn't even turn his head. "How are you doing?" I added. He wasn't listening. Suddenly he asked: "Do you know algebra?" When I told him I did, he looked at me. When we got back we caught the Eskimo drinking. The old man took the glass from his hands and drank it quickly.

Without me saying a word, my host sat by me and said: "My name's Henri Simmonet; I was the hagiographer and deputy head clerk in the Ministry of Public Works." Then he fell silent, stretched out on his bearskin, closed his eyes, and remained inert for the rest of the day.

In the evening before going to sleep he took a sheet of paper and wrote out an equation. He handed it to me, drank a bit of alcohol, and closed his eyes. Of course, Ikwah came over and grabbed the paper out of my hands. He gave me a dumbfounded look and asked me endless questions to which I gave no answer, but which annoyed me no end. To get away from him I handed him the whisky and he guzzled it down. He fell asleep almost immediately and I could study the equation. I went over to the candle and read.

PHILIPPE SOUPAULT

I left as soon as daylight entered the igloo and with one of the dogs at my heels I headed south (with the help of my compass), veering slightly to the east, and in this way came exactly to where Henri Simmonet's directions had pointed, to the Danmark Fjord—I made my way through rocks with extreme caution, afraid of landslides. I saw the remnants of a fire in a cavern where I rested for some time and where I gulped down some large eggs piled in the hollows of some rocks. Then I sought shelter for the night.

Behind a boulder I discovered a deep hollow where I hoped I could sleep in shelter from the wind, when piercing cries made me raise my head. A large number of birds came to nest in the rocks and I could observe some of them, as they were in no way frightened by my presence or by my dog who was exhausted and did not dream of chasing them. I recognized gulls and red-throated loons, but I could not make out the species of the big, noisy, and aggressive birds that were roosting in the same cave as me. I gathered some more eggs before nightfall, which came quickly.

Certain of finding eggs for my daily nourishment, I decided to explore that fjord. The shorelines were bordered by steep rocks as high as six or seven hundred meters. I walked slowly and quickly grew fatigued; the ground was hard and bumpy. By the middle of the second day, I was within sight of the fjord's shore.

I added up the kilometers I had traveled in the last eight hours, approximately, and obtained the sum of twenty-five kilometers. Fissures, sudden craters had slowed my pace.

I had been exploring the Danmark Fjord for four days when I came to the edge of an extremely deep crevice. I wanted to go around it, but I had to give that up as it seemed to extend a good distance. I slowly descended this crevice from rock to rock with some difficulty. It took me two hours to reach the bottom. I was exhausted and somewhat worried. I found myself in utter darkness and when I looked up, I could barely see any light. Nonetheless I went to sleep on a large flat stone without even thinking of lighting the candle I had in my pocket to look around.

Waking the next day, I lit my candle but noticed absolutely nothing of interest on the floor of that crevice. I saw only piles of rocks and holes in which I stuck my whole arm in and could not touch bottom. So I began to climb by clinging to the rocks. From the position of the sun, I saw that it must have been about noon when I finished that climb. I found my dog who, I don't know how, had managed to reach the other side. I immediately looked for some nests where I knew I could find nourishment.

✳

After a few hours' rest, I continued eastward. I feared the deep crevices and thus left the fjord's extreme edge, heading toward the northeast and walking more quickly than on the preceding days. That afternoon I covered thirty kilometers. The weather continued to be good and I didn't have to struggle against the wind which up until then had been my worst enemy. I saw nothing around me that caught my attention; the rocky ground was covered with flat stones.

✳

By noon of the sixth day, I saw the sea. I walked another kilometer until I arrived at the edge of a cliff and followed it, looking for any furrows that would let me descend to the foot of that cliff and reach the shore. I noted the presence of basaltic flows that formed a kind of roadway. I spent the night in a hollow; that evening I could abandon my usual nourishment, of which I was starting to tire, and fed on shellfish.

It was broad daylight when I awoke, the weather was clear, and I could follow the coastline whose geology I wanted to observe. As soon as I came down from my cave I looked around and noticed distant, gray-colored basalt pillars rising above the sea. I walked the shoreline as far as I could. I noted that the sea was very calm, and I had no fear of getting all the way to those pillars and rounding the cape that they formed.

*

A little after noon I rounded the tip of that cape and saw at some distance away some towering pillars supporting a rock and forming an immense grotto whose entrance I could see—I went into this grotto, which stretched far out to sea. At first it looked quite spacious and deep. Sunlight cast reflections across the ceiling and the walls that caused the innumerable pillars and stalactites to glitter. I proceeded with caution, for I was bedazzled and deafened. The sea lapped and the ceiling resounded with the sound of waves breaking against the walls. I didn't go to the end of that grotto. A sudden terror came over me; I began to run, out of my mind with fear.

When I reached the seashore in the open air I burst out laughing.

Monsieur, I'm asking for just one little gratuitous act, please.

PHILIPPE SOUPAULT

Squalls, flurries, the slow work of centuries always arise to demolish or disintegrate, to fissure the edifices of belief where humanity takes refuge and in whose shelter it never manages to find happiness. Religions, philosophies decompose and fall. Then the social spirit inspires new ideas or turns them to its profit. The three "stages of illusion," as Hartmann said, come to pass one by one. Doubtless they even come pell-mell, fading and returning in various sequences, according to societies and to individuals. Happiness in the present life, harmony by the will of God, in a new life, the final accord on earth between desires and acts, but only for a future humanity, enchant spirits and bend them to social law. And the collective soul leads them from one idea to the next, according to whether this one or that one adapts better to a given century, a given class, or a given individual.

FRÉDÉRIC PAULHAN

IV

———

It was a few days' hike getting back to my two companions, whom I found living on good terms, which I must admit really surprised me. Drunken and loud, Ikwah barely spoke to Henri Simmonet, who for his part regarded him absolutely as he would a bottle or a glove. And yet I thought I could discern a profound contempt for our host in everything that Ikwah said and did.

Around two o'clock one night, I woke and heard whispering, but still half asleep I was unable to understand what was being said. I lit a candle and saw Henri Simmonet and Ikwah in positions that left me in no doubt as to the nature of what they were doing. The light startled the Eskimo. In any case, I had the tact not to keep staring and went, as uncomplicated as can be, to drink a bit of whisky.

I lay down again, put out the candle, and soon after fell back asleep. For some reason, I woke later that same night. The sun had come up and it was bright enough inside the igloo that I could see my two companions still engaged.

Later Ikwah sat at the foot of my bed and told me some outlandish story, of which I could make no sense. I asked him to go away.

Since my return I'd grown less indifferent to the Eskimo's odious familiarities. Every time he spoke to me he placed his hand on my shoulder and when I didn't respond he'd give me a hard pinch. His hand gestures and his broad grin always irritated me. During my absence, he had picked up the deplorable habit of drinking constantly and in abundance, which he didn't handle well; as soon as he was drunk (which was nearly every day) he got even more boisterous than usual; he'd grab my hands, shake them, laugh loudly for no reason. If he got drunk in the evening, he would talk all night, groaning and describing his struggles with demons. He'd throw his long arms around my neck. I'd push him away but he'd hang onto me, weeping, and I'd be unable to free myself from his clutches.

One day I thought of offering him some whisky. I held the glass to his lips myself and made him drink it. Soon he fell over dead drunk and remained in that state for several hours. When he woke up again, he began vomiting.

PHILIPPE SOUPAULT

The liquor he abused poisoned him because he had no tolerance. For long hours he remained stretched out with his face to the ground, unconscious, only getting up to drink more.

I was finally at peace and could rest. After regaining my strength, I resolved to separate from that Eskimo, a precious and devoted companion during my expedition but who was irritating me.

I kept him from drinking so much for a few days and when I saw that he was able to understand what I wanted to ask him I appealed to all his devotion to accompany me on a new expedition. He accepted enthusiastically.

✷

Two days later we set out and after traveling several kilometers I told him that we had to separate. I placed some clothes on his back and told him to walk straight ahead until he reached the shore where we were to meet up again. He had brought a bottle of whisky and didn't think about the provisions I had neglected to give him. I took a different route and went back to the igloo. I wasn't worried about the Eskimo: I knew he would never return.

✷

I then started thinking a lot about the letter Dr. Raphaël Thomas Simpson, the distinguished president of the International Geographic Society of Los Angeles, had sent me before my departure. He drew my attention to the importance and interest of a scientific voyage to Greenland. Indeed, he claimed that the explorers of the polar regions, whose courage and tenacity he admired, were excellent racers but could not reasonably be considered voyagers. The president of the International Geographic Society added that despite his efforts he had been unable to uncover in their accounts the slightest bit of scientific data. He ended his letter by exhorting me to truly explore the country, to gather geological, meteorological, geographic, ethnographic observations rather than planting the flag of the Liberian Republic in some block of ice.

Trying to sort through my memories according to Dr. R. T. Simpson's method, I could not help but smile. In a flash I resolved to note the names of minerals randomly, convinced that the learned societies of the Old and New Worlds would not fail to furnish multiple explanations and that moreover no one would check on the truth of my claims. But after thinking it over I decided to note what I had seen, and especially what I would see, with complete accuracy.

Monsieur and you, Madame, I'm asking for just one little gratuitous act, please.

PHILIPPE SOUPAULT

He who does not know how to weep (for he has always repressed his inner suffering) noticed that he was in Norway. In the Faroe Islands, he witnessed a search for seabirds' nests along the steep crevices and was astonished that the three-hundred-meter rope, which dangled the explorer over the precipice, had been chosen for such sturdiness. He saw there, whatever may be said, a striking example of human goodness, and he could not believe his eyes. If it had been he who had to prepare the rope, he would have slashed it in several places so that it would break and hurl the hunter into the sea!

COMTE DE LAUTRÉAMONT

V

Mylius Erichsen Land
10 March

For several days Henri hasn't spoken a word to me and I've said nothing to him. I still smile when I think of R. T. Simpson's letter. My exploration of the Danmark Fjord would have led me to travel through the region, if the man I was living with wasn't Henri Simmonet.

Besides, the ill success of this expedition puts me off all the others, and I am determined from now on to live from day to day.

14 March

Silence still reigns over this dwelling. I'm constantly watching my companion. He, on the other hand, barely looks at me.

The wind today is blowing violently, and the dogs fought tonight.

16 March

Yesterday evening, for the first time since my second return, Henri Simmonet deigned to speak to me. True, it was to ask me for the whisky bottle. He thanked me vaguely, very vaguely even, and fell back asleep. I'm noting some meteorological observations and sewing up my clothes.

3 April

I've stopped going outside.

Henri is talking to me a bit.

5 April

Yesterday evening I tore up the notes I had been taking for the president of the International Geographic Society of Los Angeles.

6 April

Neither of us goes outside and we rarely speak. Tonight, a dog that for some reason has not yet died of hunger came to scratch and howl at the plank that closes off the entrance tunnel.

7 April

Today I again questioned Henri, who claims to have forgotten everything.

I discovered under some bearskins a footlocker, whose lock I broke off. It contained a few shirts, some nails, a photograph of Henri, a book, *Carpentry for Beginners*, a mirror, and some sheets of paper.

17 April

Five or six days ago I showed Henri Simmonet the photograph that I found in the footlocker. He said nothing at first, but soon I saw him laugh, then shrug his shoulders and toss the photograph away: "I won't even rip it up," he murmured. Intrigued, I asked him why he was acting that way: "My dearest friend," he answered, "at that time there was an individual named Jules Poidevin, aged thirty-five. One day he was in the home of a married couple named Lezi, ironmongers on rue Le Peletier; he had brought a revolver, checked the mechanism in front of the persons present, then laughed and pointed the weapon at Madame Lezi: 'Watch out,' he cried, 'I'm going to kill you!' That very instant a shot was fired and Madame Lezi was struck in her right temple and fell, mortally wounded. My friend was arrested and declared that he had forgotten the gun was loaded."

Closing his eyes Henri added:

"Is that grotesque enough?"

I'm now following my companion's example, who barely speaks to me anymore and stays in bed.

23 April

I noticed yesterday that my companion eats with resignation. I used to think that he took pleasure in drinking, but I see that's not at all the case. He drinks the way invalids take medicine they're tired of taking.

27 April

Getting up to urinate Henri seriously injured himself. He stepped on an open tin can and cut his big toe to the bone.

His reaction to doing so astounded me and I believe that it is indeed astounding. He seemed bored but like a man tickled by a fly.

I have begun to clean the igloo because the stench of decay has gotten too strong. I asked my companion to get up so that I could clean the filth he was lying in. He got up, shrugged, then lay down on my bed.

1 May

The igloo is cleaner now, but I still have not gone outside. The wind must be very violent because I've heard it whistling for several days now. Henri still hasn't spoken.

5 May

I used to think that he was sad and that his silence was due to this sadness alone. I found out today that I was wrong. I am not sure why, but I'm convinced that Henri Simmonet doesn't know the meaning of sadness.

I asked my companion several questions today and now realize, a bit too late no doubt, my indiscretion. But Henri Simmonet is content to smile and keep silent—never once have I seen him get angry.

30 May

After an extended silence we begin to speak again. Lack of air and exercise has completely taken away my appetite. But I drink a lot, even too much, and I have absolutely made up my mind to taper off.

13 June

While leafing this morning through *Carpentry for Beginners* I found a newspaper clipping:

MAN WITH RIFLE

A stakeout operation is being conducted in the 13th Arrondissement where for the past several days an individual who has eluded capture has been randomly firing a rifle at passersby. Monsieur Louis Borne, head of the prefecture of police, almost fell victim to this mysterious criminal. He was riding in a victoria along Boulevard de la Gare when a bullet shattered the windowpane and passed a few centimeters from his face.

A gratuitous act, goddammit.

PHILIPPE SOUPAULT

All the objects from the show—ephemeris, steel rod, rosary, box of straws, crystal sphere, reddened straw, die, star code, magnifying glass, willow branch, sheet of ivory, easel, mica box, coal sack, and perforated tin emptied of embers—were put carefully back by Noël into the flexible basket, which was soon refastened to the shoulders of Hopsus who was set back on the ground.

RAYMOND ROUSSEL

———

Below the 81st parallel North.
I believe I stayed with him for over two years.

Waking one night I suddenly realized that I was beginning to love him. I felt that I had to leave.

I left.

Winter had been over for two weeks.

I drove my sled toward the Danmark Fjord, to reach the seashore—I recognized the route I had once taken and decided to jettison the tin cans, now needless and cumbersome.

I placed them in the shelter of a deep cave, hidden by rocks but which I could easily find again.

I am now aboard the schooner "L'Alliance," which picked me up on the beach two days ago. A storm had tossed it northeast of Greenland and as it passed by it saw my signal.

There are ten or so men on the ship, among whom was one of my old friends I'd known in Roscoff, Thomas Le Guellec; he spoke well of me to the captain. Naturally that man took me for a madman and smiles when he passes me.

In his cabin I found a collection of wonderful maps of Oceania.

Justin Vicari is a poet, translator, and critical theorist, largely self-taught. His books include *In Search of Lost Joy* (2018), *Marks of Toil* (2016), *Nicolas Winding Refn and the Violence of Art* (2015), and *Mad Muses and the Early Surrealists* (2012). He has also translated works by Octave Mirbeau, J.-K. Huysmans, and François Emmanuel. He lives in the greater Pittsburgh area.

Jonathan P. Eburne lives in central Pennsylvania, where he is a professor of Comparative Literature, English, and French and Francophone studies at the Pennsylvania State University. He is the author of the forthcoming book *Exploded Views*, as well as *Outsider Theory: Intellectual Histories of Unorthodox Ideas* (2018), which received the 2020 James Russell Lowell Prize from the Modern Language Association, and *Surrealism and the Art of Crime* (2008); additionally, he is co-editor of four other books. Eburne is also part of the team launching a new nonprofit bookstore and culture space called The Print Factory (www.printfactorybellefonte.org).